Rubix Ruckus Reubenstein Visits the Farm

RUBIX

RUBIX RUCKUS REUBENSTEIN VISITS THE FARM

Author and Photographer
Jennifer Nitz

Illustrated by Kit Jagoda

RubiJen
Want to give Rubix a howl? Contact him at www.rubixruckus.wix.com/rubix or find Rubix Ruckus Reubenstein on Facebook!
ISBN: 978-0-9913418-1-8

ACKNOWLEDGEMENTS

Rubix and I would like to extend a huge thank you to Jack, Bruce, and Barley, who generously shared your Mom's geeky brain and computer to help assemble our book, asking for nothing in return but vegan ice cream! Big thanks to my Dad, who once again offered his skills and support to get this book looking it's best! Much gratitude to Bonnie Goodman of Mordam Art for your support and technical skills.

Special thanks to Kit Jagoda of River's Wish Animal Sanctuary for taking the time out of your busy schedule to create the beautiful illustrations. Read more about Kit and River's Wish Animal Sanctuary at the end of the book.

Much love and thanks to Rubix Ruckus Reubenstein, who's childlike approach to life inspired our second book! You continue to teach me the best way to look at the world, and you bring joy to those who are lucky enough to be a part of your life. May all your dreams come true!

Yay! We're going on a car ride! We are going to visit a very special place! We are going to help at a Farm Sanctuary!

Sanctuary means safe place, so the Farm Sanctuary is a safe new home for animals who were living on a farm. We're here!

Oh my goodness, look at everybody! All new and different friends. Who do you see? I see goats, and chickens, and cows, and llamas, and pigs, and sheep!

Let's go meet everybody
and learn all about them!

We love to run, and jump, and play! We can jump over 5 feet high!

We are called kids when we are babies, girls are does or nannys, boys are bucks or billies, and we can all have beards. A group of us is a herd, welcome to the herd, Rubix!

Thank you! I love to run and jump and play too! We will have so much fun together!

Tracks! I wonder who made these. The snow is melting so fast it's hard to tell. The snow is aready gone on so much of the Sanctuary.

Which way did
he go, George?
I don't know. Which
way did he go, Walter?

Hi sheep friends! Hi Rubix,
we are happy to meet you!

Thank you, I am happy to
meet you too! I would like to
learn all about you.

Oh, goody! We love to socialize! We bleat while you bark.

We can see behind us without turning our heads! We grow wool like you grow fur. Our babies are called lambs, girls are ewes and boys are rams. A group of us is called a flock, welcome to the flock, Rubix!

Thank you! I love to socialize
too, and will come back soon!

Golly, this place is fun! Hi Henry!
Hi Bergh! Did you see that?

Hi Chicken friends! Hi Rubix, it's good to meet you! Thank you, you are even more bright and colorful in person!

Thank you, our feathers have all different colors and patterns. We are the closest living relative to the dinasaur Tyrannosaurus Rex! Our babies are chicks, and we can talk to them while they are still in their eggs! Then we grow up to be roosters which are the boys, and hens which are the girls. A group of us is a flock, welcome to the flock, Rubix!

Wow, what interesting stories you have! Thank you, I feel so lucky to know you, and will come back to learn more!

Gosh, I knew I would have fun, but I am learning so much too! Sanctuaries are wonderful places, and I am thankful everyone is safe here!

Hi Oliver! Hi Rubix, thank you for joining me on my walk. I like to go for walks too, it is a special treat to join you, everyone is so unique here.

We are all different, but enjoy being together. I am a male pig which is a boar, girls are sows, and our babies are piglets. We are very smart and love to socialize too!

We roll in the mud to cool ourselves and protect our skin from the sun. We also love to swim! Let's go grunt with Boris, grunt is how we talk or bark.

Boris is taking a nap, I'll watch over the chickens!
We have a very strong sense of smell. Boris will know
if someone is here to hurt the chickens, just like he
knows you came over.

Welcome to the Sanctuary, Rubix! We hope you can stay a
long time! Thank you, me too!

Aw, Boris! Stop it, that tickles!

Hi llama friends! Hi Rubix, we are happy you are here! Thank you, I am so happy to be here visiting and learning about everyone!

We are members of the camel family and can grow up to 6 feet tall. Girls are hembra, boys are macho, and babies are cria (KREE-uh). We like to hum, and also use our tails, ears, and other sounds to communicate. Our eyes have sunshields built in and we can close them when we need to!

We are sacred to the Andean people and called silent brothers. We may be silent, but we love the company of others, and will defend our herd!

Welcome to the herd, Rubix! Thank you, it is a pleasure to be in your herd!

I'm so excited, I have to run!!

Cow friends, hi! Hi Rubix, it's good to see you! Thank you, I have been hearing all about your friends here, now it's time learn all about you! We are all friends here, everyone is special with their own stories that we like to hear too.

I have something stuck in my TOOF!

We can smell you from 6 miles away, and can see almost all around without turning our heads! We will run and jump when we get excited or learn something new. We love our families and a cow will walk for miles to find her calf.

We are cattle, boys are bulls and girls are heifers until they have a calf, then they are cows. We are held sacred in several religions.

A group of us is called a herd, welcome to the herd, Rubix!
Thank you, it is an honor to be one of your herd!

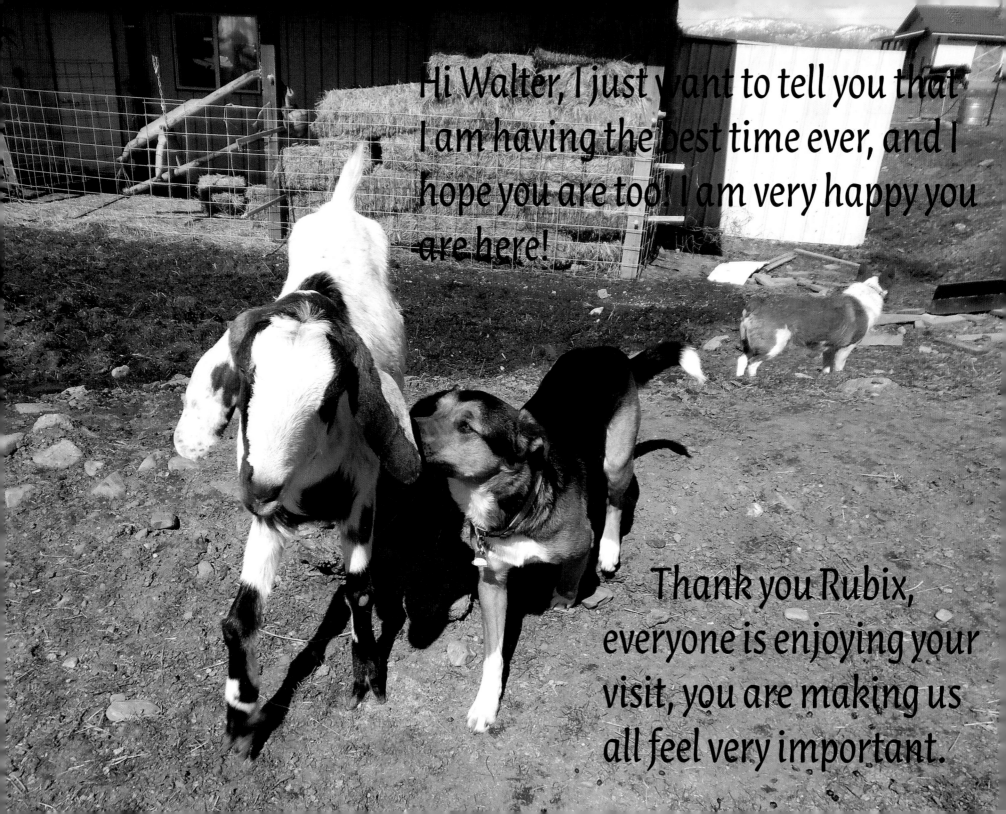

Hi Walter, I just want to tell you that I am having the best time ever, and I hope you are too! I am very happy you are here!

Thank you Rubix, everyone is enjoying your visit, you are making us all feel very important.

I am so glad to hear that, because
everyone here is important!

There was a shuffling sound on top of the barn and everyone turned to see crow friend!

Crow said, "My favorite time is when I get to perch up here and watch this Farm family live together. Through everyone's similarities and differences, everyone wants the same thing: to be happy and healthy, and live in peace!"

Oh, look! Here is some fresh grass, I can imagine how fresh and green the Sanctuary is going to be very soon!

Hi Rubix, it's a lot of fun having someone new to explore with. I agree, Oliver. It's been fun learning that everyone enjoys the same things I do. Yes we do, we didn't have this freedom on the farms we came from. We are the lucky ones that get to be at a Sanctuary.

I'm glad you are one of the lucky ones, and hope everyone gets to be the lucky ones someday!

Hooray! It's time to feed the chickens, and I am going to help! It's a lot of work making sure everyone stays healthy at a Sanctuary. The people who live here with everybody are just as important, with all their own stories, as all our new friends!

This has been such a memorable visit. It's time to curl up with my good friend, Barry who gets to live at the Sanctuary too!

I am going to dream about all our new friends, and about all their friends and families too! Everyone should be able to live in places they can call Sanctuary!

Dedicated to Sue Eakins of New Dawn MT Farm Sanctuary

Rubix and I were caretakers at New Dawn MT Farm Sanctuary for several months. Our experience was the inspiration for this book, and is where the majority of the story takes place.

Sue was a social worker in Texas when she started feeling conflicted about calling one animal "pet" and another "food". She decided to do some research and realized if she truly did love animals, she could not eat or use them also. Sue adopted the vegan lifestyle, and she and her husband decided to buy land in Montana, and open a Sanctuary as a way to give back to the animals. The Sanctuary evolved into many things, and Sue became an inspiration to so many, including me. She had an "awakening", and acted on it, truly living her life with purpose, and teaching others through example and education.

Sadly, Sue succcomed to cancer on November 9, 2014. Sue's life impacted so many in a positive way, and is remembered in the way she wanted to be, as a teacher and voice for the animals!

Get to know Sue! Watch https://www.youtube.com/watch?v=BR5tXMlVVNg, and read https://missoulian.com/life-styles/territory/sanctuary-from-slaughter-florence-woman-takes-in-farm-animals/article_0ca53974-2e23-11df-999d-001cc4c002e0.html

RIVER'S WISH

ANIMAL SANCTUARY

SAVING LIVES THROUGH RESCUE, EDUCATION & ADVOCACY

River's Wish Animal Sanctuary rests on 65 acres on a plateau in Spokane County, Washington. This 501c3 nonprofit provides refuge for formerly farmed animals and those who have no place to go.

The mission is to save lives through rescue, education and advocacy. Through our sanctuary based humane education program we advocate for compassionate life choices and we offer workshops connecting art and animals.

Farm Animal Sanctuaries provide a safe home for animals familiarly known as farm animals. Some of these animals were court ordered, some were freely given up, others escaped, and some former farms have decided to become Sanctuaries. Whatever the reason, we are thankful to the compassionate people that recognize these animals as individuals deserving of and needing a safe place, and providing that for them.

To find a Farm Animal Sanctuary, you can go to, www.vegan.com/Sanctuaries, this list also contains animals rescued from laboratories. The list is continuously updated.